My Secret Unicorn

A Winter Wish

Leaving Carla and Anna to go back
to sleep, she went downstairs. A heavy frost had
fallen in the night — so heavy that Lauren left footprints
in it as she trudged down the path to Twilight's stable.

He whinnied when he saw her.

"I'm really sorry I didn't come out last night," she told him,
going into the stable and putting her arms around his neck.
"Carla and Anna wanted to have a midnight feast." She bit her
lip. "Actually, I think it's going to be too risky to try to come
flying while they're sharing a room with me. What if they wake
up and find I'm gone?"

Twilight stared at her.

Lauren wished she could turn him into a unicorn
so she could really talk to him. "I don't know what to do,"
she told him. "I know you love flying but I just don't know
if I should risk it."

My Secret Unicorn

Unicorn

A Winter Wish

Linda Chapman
Illustrated by Biz Hull

Cover Illustration by Andrew Farley

AN
APPLE
PAPERBACK

SCHOLASTIC INC.
New York   Toronto   London   Auckland   Sydney
Mexico City   New Delhi   Hong Kong   Buenos Aires

To Amany Lily — forever

ISBN 0-439-70125-2

12   11   10   9   8   7   6   5   4   3   5   6   7   8   9/0

Printed in the U.S.A.   40

First Scholastic printing, December 2004

CHAPTER

One

Lauren stroked Twilight's dapple-gray neck, her breath misting in the cold air. "Almost there," she spoke softly. Now that it was December, the woods seemed very quiet when it started to get dark.

Twilight nodded. Anyone watching would have thought he was just an ordinary gray pony walking down an overgrown woodland trail — but he wasn't.

When Lauren said the words of the Turning Spell, he transformed into a magical unicorn.

My secret unicorn, Lauren thought, with a familiar thrill of excitement.

The path came out into a clearing. Even though it was winter, the short grass was dotted with star-shaped purple flowers. Fireflies danced through the still air, and around the edge of the clearing, unusual pinkish-gray rocks of rose quartz shone softly in the fading light.

Lauren quickly dismounted. "We can't stay long. You know Dad gets worried if I'm out when it's dark. But there's something I really want to do."

She took off her hat and, tucking her long blond hair behind her ears, said the spell that would turn Twilight into his magical form.

> *"Twilight Star, Twilight Star,*
> *Twinkling high above so far.*
> *Shining light, shining bright,*
> *Will you grant my wish tonight?*
> *Let my little horse forlorn*
> *Be at last a unicorn."*

With a purple flash, Twilight became a snowy-white unicorn. He whinnied and tossed his long mane. His silver horn gleamed.

"Twilight!" Lauren exclaimed, hugging him.

Twilight nuzzled her. "Hello, Lauren. So, what would you like to do? Don't you want to go flying?"

"Oh, yes, of course, but first I want to use your magic to see if Carla and Anna have gotten the Christmas cards I sent them," Lauren replied. "I've invited them to come and stay during the holidays."

Carla and Anna had been Lauren's best friends when she lived in the city. Although she'd kept in touch with them by phone, she hadn't seen them for eight months — not since her family had moved to the country.

"Well, let's have a look," Twilight said.

He bent his head toward one of the rose quartz rocks. As a unicorn, he had many magical powers. One of them allowed him to use the special rocks to see what was happening elsewhere in the world.

Lauren was about to kneel down to watch when she suddenly frowned. "Twilight, you will be all right if we do this, won't you? I don't want to make you sick."

Twilight's magical powers were only supposed to be used for helping people. If Lauren used them too much just for fun, he became weak and sick.

"I'll be fine," Twilight reassured her. "We're only going to have a quick look, and you do want to see your friends." He touched his horn to the surface of the rose quartz. "Carla and Anna, Lauren's friends!" he declared.

There was a bright purple flash and a cloud of mist swirled over the rock. As it cleared, the surface of the rock shone and

a picture appeared. It was like seeing a
reflection in a pool.

"There they are!" Lauren gasped, seeing
her friends sitting in Carla's kitchen. Carla's
wavy red hair had been cut short since
Lauren had last seen her but Anna looked
just the same with her long black hair tied
back in a ponytail. They were talking
excitedly and looking at two Christmas
cards, handmade with gold and silver
glitter. Lauren recognized them as the cards
she had sent.

"Your friends look really nice," Twilight
commented. "Do they like horses as well?"

"Oh, yes," Lauren replied. "They love
them, although they don't go for regular
riding lessons. Carla knows how to ride a

little because she's had some lessons at summer camp, but Anna's only been on a couple of trail rides." She leaned closer to the rock, eager to hear what her friends were saying. The faint buzz of Carla's and Anna's voices became clearer.

"It'll be so cool!" Carla was saying. "It'll be really good to see Lauren."

"And her pony, Twilight," Anna put in.

Twilight gave a proud nicker.

Carla nodded. "I'm going to get my mom to call Lauren's mom tonight to arrange it."

"Me, too," Anna said, her brown eyes shining. "Let's try to go as soon as school ends for the holidays."

Lauren sat back and their voices faded

to a buzz again. "They're going to come," she said happily. It would be fantastic to see them again and she couldn't wait to show off Twilight! "It's going to be hard not to tell them the truth about you," she admitted.

She wasn't allowed to tell anyone Twilight's secret — not even her mom and dad. The only two people who did know about him were her friend Michael, who lived in the city and had a unicorn of his own, and Mrs. Fontana, the woman who ran the local bookstore. It had been Mrs. Fontana who had told Lauren that all around the world there are unicorns, disguised as small gray ponies, who are each looking for a child to be their special secret unicorn friend. If it hadn't been for Mrs. Fontana, Lauren would never have discovered that Twilight was a unicorn in disguise.

Twilight looked thoughtful. "I know you can't tell Carla and Anna about me, but we can still have lots of fun going for rides together."

Lauren grinned. "You're right, Twilight. That will be great!"

"Let's go flying now," said Twilight.

"You bet!" said Lauren, and she jumped up onto Twilight's back. Taking two strides, he leaped upward into the sky.

It was dark enough now for them not to be seen. The frosty air stung Lauren's cheeks and she was glad to have her thick coat and gloves. Lauren's hair flew out behind her as they flew over the treetops that were dusted with a light, shimmering cover of snow. "It's beginning to feel really Christmassy," she said. "I can't wait until school ends on Friday."

"Then we'll get to spend lots of time together," Twilight said happily.

Lauren nodded. "It'll be so much fun." She loved vacations when she could spend hours with Twilight — talking to him, grooming him, riding him, and, of course, flying with him at night.

At the edge of the woods, Lauren turned Twilight back into a pony by saying the magical words of the Undoing Spell. As she trotted him up the trail that led back to the farm, she saw her dad waiting for her.

"I was just starting to get worried," Mike Foster said. "You know I don't like you being out in the dark, Lauren."

"Sorry, Dad," Lauren said.

"It's all right," Mr. Foster replied, patting Twilight. "Just try and be back a little earlier next time. I know you're sensible but the woods *are* more dangerous in winter. Snow can fall very suddenly and if that happened, you might get lost."

Lauren nodded. "I promise I won't stay out late again and I'll be careful."

Her dad smiled. "Good girl."

Lauren dismounted and stroked Twilight's neck. She knew her dad was

right — the woods *were* more dangerous in winter — but she also knew that Twilight would always look after her.

She led him up to his warm stable and kissed his nose. "I always feel safe when I'm with you," she told him.

CHAPTER

Two

"Hey, you two! You'll never guess what." Lauren gasped, running up to her school friends Mel Cassidy and Jessica Parker the next morning. "I've got some great news!" She paused to catch her breath.

"Whatever your news is, it's not going to beat mine!" Mel announced. "My mom said she'll take us to the Christmas fun show at Fox Run Riding School. I went last year and it was totally awesome! It's on Christmas Eve. There are no jumping classes or anything like that — just lots of gymkhana games, and everyone dresses up their ponies with tinsel."

"Wow!" Lauren exclaimed, her own news going completely out of her head. "That sounds great!"

"Mel says you have to go in teams of three people," Jessica put in. "We can be a team all together!"

They grinned at one another.

"Let's all practice at my house on Monday," Mel said.

"Yeah!" Lauren replied. She and Mel lived on neighboring farms, and Jessica and

her stepsister, Samantha, kept Sandy, their
new pony, at Mel's so it would be easy to
meet up.

Just then, the bell rang.

"What were you going to tell us,
Lauren?" Jessica asked as they made their
way to their classroom.

"My friends Carla and Anna are coming
to stay during the holidays," Lauren said,

remembering her own exciting news. Carla's and Anna's parents had phoned the night before and it was all arranged. Carla's dad was going to drive the two girls to the farm on Saturday and Anna's dad was going to pick them up on Wednesday morning.

"How long are they staying?" Mel asked.

"Until Christmas Eve," Lauren told her. "But they're leaving early in the morning so I'll be able to come to the show." She smiled happily. "I just know you're going to like them."

She broke off as the classroom door opened and their teacher walked in. They hastily sat down at their desks and the class began.

★ ★ ★

"So, how was school today?" Mrs. Foster asked that afternoon when she picked up Lauren and Max, Lauren's six-year-old brother.

"Hard." Max sighed deeply. "We never get to do anything fun anymore."

Lauren grinned at her mom. Now that Max was in first grade, he was always complaining about how much work he had to do.

"Never mind," Mrs. Foster said. "It'll be the holidays soon." She switched on the turn signal and pulled off the main road.

"Where are we going?" Lauren asked curiously.

"To Mrs. Fontana's bookstore," her

mom replied. "I wanted to look for some Christmas presents."

Lauren was pleased. She loved Mrs. Fontana's old-fashioned store with its piles of colorful books. She also loved seeing Mrs. Fontana. *I wonder if I'll get a chance to talk to her about Twilight,* she thought.

Mrs. Fontana was halfway up a ladder when they arrived. "Hello there," she called.

"Hi, Mrs. Fontana," Lauren's mom replied as Walter, Mrs. Fontana's black-and-white terrier, scampered over to them. "We thought we'd come in to browse."

"Feel free." Mrs.

Fontana's face creased into a warm smile. "There are some new pony books in the children's section, Lauren."

Leaving her mom to look in the cookbook section, Lauren headed to the far end of the store.

Max was busy playing with Walter, and Lauren waited to see if Mrs. Fontana would come find her. Sure enough, a few minutes later, the store owner came into the children's section. "How's Twilight?" she asked.

"He's fine," Lauren replied.

Their eyes met and Mrs. Fontana dropped her voice. "Have you been out flying much?"

"Every night," Lauren whispered.

Mrs. Fontana smiled. "It should snow soon and then you'll really have fun. I remember the first time I flew in the snow. It was wonderful." For a moment she looked lost in memories. She shook her head and focused on Lauren again. "Enjoy it," she said softly. "I promise you it'll be an experience you won't forget."

"Lauren!"

Hearing her mom, Lauren quickly turned around. "Yes?" she said, trying to look as normal as possible.

Mrs. Foster came into the children's section. "Why don't you choose a couple of books for Carla and Anna?"

"OK, thanks. That's a good idea!" Lauren replied.

"Carla and Anna?" Mrs. Fontana echoed as Mrs. Foster left to go back to the adult section, and Lauren started looking at the shelf of pony books.

"They were my best friends when I lived in the city," Lauren explained. "They're coming to stay on Saturday and we're going to do lots of Christmassy things." She felt a rush of excitement. "I can't wait to see them! We've been friends since we were four."

"That's good," Mrs. Fontana said. "Friends are very important." Her bright blue eyes studied Lauren for a moment. "All friends — old ones, new ones, special ones, even four-legged ones. They all have a part to play in our lives."

Lauren wasn't sure what she meant. "Yes," she agreed hesitantly.

Mrs. Fontana smiled. "Well, I'm sure you'll have a wonderful time." She spoke more briskly. "Now, what sort of books do they like?"

With Mrs. Fontana's help, Lauren chose pony stories for Carla and Anna. Mrs. Foster paid and then she, Lauren, and Max went back out to the car.

As they drove home, her mom put on a tape of Christmas songs. Gazing at the decorated store fronts flashing by in a festive blur, Lauren felt very happy. With the fun show and her friends' visit to look forward to, this Christmas looked like it was going to be the best she'd ever had!

CHAPTER

Three

By Friday, Lauren was very excited. Just one more day and then Carla and Anna would be here! She'd been busy planning their visit all week. Each day they were going to muck out and ride Twilight in the morning, and then in the afternoon they would clean tack and ride again. She also wanted to do lots of Christmas things,

like making decorations and Christmas
cards and baking.

"I want it to be just perfect," she told
Mel as they rode through the woods on
Friday after school. Jessica wasn't with
them because she had gone to stay at her
grandmother's for the night. "I think we'll
have a really horsey day tomorrow," Lauren
continued. "And we might make some
Christmas gingerbread in the afternoon.
We can decorate it with — "

"The Christmas candies you bought
with your mom," Mel finished, sounding
slightly fed up.

Lauren stared at her friend in surprise,
taken aback.

"Sorry," Mel said quickly. "I didn't mean to be impatient. It's just, well . . . you have been talking about it a lot."

Lauren realized it was her turn to apologize. "Sorry. It's just that I can't wait to see them. They're my oldest friends!"

"I know," Mel said.

"I really want you to meet them," Lauren told her. "Why don't you come over in the morning, then you can see them as soon as they arrive?"

"OK," Mel replied.

Lauren smiled happily. She was sure Mel would like Carla and Anna as much as she did. She glanced up the wide sandy trail. "Let's canter."

"I'll race you to the oak tree," Mel challenged.

"Come on, Twilight!" Lauren gasped as Mel's light gray pony, Shadow, set off. Twilight didn't need any encouragement. Plunging forward, he caught up with Shadow and the two ponies cantered side by side along the trail.

★ ★ ★

That night, Lauren made Twilight's bed especially deep and warm. "I won't be able to come flying tonight," she told him. "I've got to get everything ready for Carla and Anna. You don't mind, do you, boy?"

She wondered if he would be upset but he just bumped her gently with his nose, and Lauren knew it was his way of saying that he understood.

"Lauren!" her mom shouted from the house. "Supper!"

"Coming!" Lauren called back.

Going up the path to the house, she imagined what Carla and Anna were doing right now. Probably talking on the phone. That's what she would have been doing if she were still living in the city. Lauren smiled. Her life had certainly changed a lot in the last eight months. Back then, she had spent her time shopping, playing at friends' houses, going to different classes — riding, gym, swimming. Now that she lived in the country, her life was totally different. She spent most of her time with Twilight, and she was hardly ever out of her riding clothes.

I wonder what Carla and Anna will think? she wondered.

The following morning, Lauren paced up and down the kitchen. Going to the window, she checked the driveway for about the fortieth time. No sign of her friends yet. Carla's dad, who was driving them there, had said they would probably

arrive at about 11:00. But it was 11:15
already. Where were they?

"I'm sure they'll be here soon," Mrs.
Foster said, joining her at the window.
"Don't worry."

"I just want them to get here," Lauren
said.

Outside, Max was playing fetch with
Buddy, his young Bernese mountain dog.
Buddy was leaping around in the puddles
on the driveway, his enormous paws
splashing muddy water everywhere.

"That dog." Mrs. Foster sighed, shaking
her head in affectionate exasperation. "He
seems to get bigger every day!"

"He'll be as big as Twilight soon."
Lauren grinned. She glanced down the

driveway. "Mom!" She gasped. "They're here!"

A sleek black car pulled up in front of the house. Carla and Anna were in the back together, looking out the window. They waved excitedly as Lauren ran outside.

Carla threw open the car door. "Hi, Lauren!" she cried.

She was interrupted by a massive *woof* as Buddy bounded toward the car, ears flapping and mouth open.

Carla gasped and slammed the door shut.

Delighted at seeing guests, Buddy jumped up at the car, standing on his back legs and peering in the window.

Lauren saw the alarm on her friends' faces. "It's OK. He's just really friendly!" she cried, hurrying toward the car. "Get down, Buddy!" she scolded, grabbing his collar. She hoped Mr. Price, Carla's dad, wouldn't mind the muddy paw prints over his fancy car.

She struggled to hold on to Buddy's collar.

"Stop being bad," Max said to him.

Just then, Mrs. Foster came out of the house. "Oh, Buddy!"

Mr. Price got out of the car. "Wow! That dog looks like a handful. Is he a guard dog?"

"Guard dog?" Lauren echoed, grinning at her mom.

"This is Max's puppy," Mrs. Foster explained with a smile.

"He's named Buddy," Max added, going over and ruffling Buddy's ears.

Carla and Anna got out of the car. "I thought he was going to attack us," Anna joked.

"Hi, boy," Carla said to him.

Buddy pulled away from Lauren and trotted over to say hello. Carla reached out to stroke him but then hastily pulled her hand back. "Yuck! He's all muddy!"

Buddy pushed his head against Carla's blue jeans. "Oh, no, my new jeans! They've got mud on them now!" She gasped.

Lauren stared at her. Since when had it mattered if her jeans got muddy?

"I'm sorry, Carla," Mrs. Foster said, hurrying forward and hauling Buddy away. "I'll run your jeans through the washing machine later. Now, why don't you all come inside and Buddy can stay out here?"

They all trooped toward the house.

"What's that smell?" Anna asked, wrinkling her nose.

"That's just the pigs," Mrs. Foster told her. "They're in the far field but when the wind is in the wrong direction you get the occasional whiff of them."

Anna, Carla, and Mr. Price exchanged alarmed glances and hurried inside the farmhouse.

While the adults had coffee, Lauren gave her friends a tour of the house. "This is the living room and this is the dining room," she explained. "And over here's the sun porch."

Neither Anna nor Carla spoke. It was as if now that the initial excitement of meeting was over, none of them knew quite what to say to one another.

As Lauren led the way upstairs, the awkward silence seemed to lengthen. She began to feel nervous. What if the silence went on and on for the next four days?

She shouldn't have worried. When they reached her room, Carla and Anna both drew in a breath.

"Wow!" said Carla, looking at the light room with its sloping ceiling, wide window seat, and walls covered with posters of ponies. "This is a really pretty room, Lauren."

"And look!" Anna said, going to the window. "Is that Twilight?"

"Yes," Lauren replied.

"He's gorgeous," Carla exclaimed, joining Anna at the window.

"Can we go see him, Lauren?" Anna pleaded.

"Oh, yes please," Carla begged.

Lauren felt a rush of relief. It looked as if her friends were excited to be here after all. She decided to tease them. "Well," she said, as if she were thinking it over. "I don't know. . . . " She broke off with a squeal as Carla tickled her. "OK, you can see him! You can see him!"

"Right now?" Carla demanded.

"Right now," Lauren gasped, trying to escape from Carla's tickling fingers.

Carla grinned and stopped tickling her. "Come on, then! What are you waiting for?"

"Come on, yourself," Lauren retorted and together the three of them raced down the stairs.

CHAPTER

Four

T his is Twilight!" Lauren said proudly. Hearing their voices, Twilight had come to the gate and now he reached over it, blowing gently on Carla's and Anna's hands.

"I can't believe he's yours, Lauren!" Anna gasped, her eyes wide.

Carla stroked his cheek. "He's so beautiful!"

"Can we ride him?" Anna asked.

"Of course!" Lauren replied. "I groomed him this morning so we can ride right away." She looked at their nice clothes. "But do you need to get changed first?"

"Yes, we'd better," Carla agreed. "I

don't want to get my new jeans dirty —
well, any dirtier than they already are," she
added ruefully, looking down at the muddy
streaks Buddy had left.

"And I should change my shoes," Anna
said with a glance at her pink sneakers.

They went inside.

"So, what's school like?" Lauren asked
as Carla and Anna unpacked some older
clothes. "How is everyone?"

"The same as always," Carla replied.
"Daniel Armstrong and Mark Siddons are
still driving me crazy. I had to sit next to
them this term and they kept kicking my
chair and throwing paper wads at me."

"So nothing's changed there, then,"
Lauren said. "They are *so* annoying!"

"They're not that bad," Anna protested. "I do judo with Daniel now and he can be really nice."

"Anna loves Daniel!" Lauren and Carla said at the same time. They grinned at each other.

"I don't!" Anna cried.

Lauren felt happiness fizz up inside her. It was wonderful being back with her old friends again. As they got changed, they told her all the news. There was hardly a second's pause in the conversation, and it was almost as if they hadn't been away from one another at all.

They ran back to the field and Lauren tacked Twilight up.

Anna tried to help by doing up the

bridle but she fastened the throatlash to the noseband strap.

"That's not quite right, Anna," Lauren said quickly.

"Oh." Anna looked flustered.

Lauren did the straps up correctly.

"Does this go on like this, Lauren?" Carla asked, putting the saddlepad on Twilight's back the wrong way around.

"No, it's backward," Lauren told her. She turned it around and then put Twilight's saddle on. "The pad has to pull up into the gullet of the saddle like this," she told them. "It shouldn't press flat against his back."

Anna looked at her. "You know lots about horses now, Lauren."

Lauren was surprised. She hadn't really thought about it before, but back in the city she'd only ridden ponies in riding school and she'd never looked after one on her own before. She guessed that she *had* learned a lot since she'd gotten Twilight.

They took Twilight into the field. Lauren rode first. "He's really good," she told her friends. She trotted around a few times and then popped over a small jump before riding back to the gate.

"Can I have a turn?" Anna asked eagerly. She put on Lauren's hat and mounted, leaning forward nervously in the saddle.

"Do you want me to lead you?" Lauren asked.

Anna nodded gratefully. "Yes, please."

Lauren led Anna and Twilight around the field. "Try sitting back a little," she suggested. "It'll feel more comfy."

Anna eased backward a few inches but still clung on to Twilight's mane. He walked calmly, and gradually Anna started to relax.

"This is fun," she said after five minutes. "But I should probably let Carla have a turn now."

They went back to the gate and Carla and Anna swapped places. Carla looked much more confident, although she held her reins tightly. "I don't need to be led," she told Lauren. "I'll be fine. I had some more riding lessons when I was at camp this summer." She kicked Twilight. He jumped forward and she grabbed the reins

even tighter. Twilight threw his head back
as the bit banged against his teeth.

"Steady!" Carla's voice rose in alarm.

"You're holding the reins too tightly,"
Lauren said.

Carla looked annoyed. "You don't have
to tell me how to ride, Lauren!" She

loosened her hold and Twilight walked forward. But as they rode around the field, Carla's fingers crept up the reins again.

Lauren bit her lip. She knew Carla hated being corrected but she didn't want Twilight to be unhappy, either. To her relief, he seemed to wink as he went past, as if to say, *It's OK, don't worry, I'm fine.*

"He's great!" Carla exclaimed. "Can I try a trot?"

Lauren nodded and Carla urged Twilight into a trot.

He moved forward smoothly. Carla pulled at his mouth a little but he didn't seem to care. He trotted around the field, his ears pricked and his tail swinging.

Suddenly, there was a whinny behind

them. Lauren looked around. Mel was riding toward them on Shadow.

"Mel! Hi!" she called, hurrying toward her. "Come meet Carla and Anna. Carla's riding Twilight, and Anna's by the gate."

Mel rode over. "Hi," she said shyly to Anna.

Anna smiled back. "Hello."

Carla rode over. "Hi, I'm Carla."

"I'm Mel," said Mel. "I live next door to Lauren."

"Your pony's pretty," Anna told her.

Mel smiled. "Thanks. His name is Shadow."

Carla frowned. "That's a weird name for such a light-colored pony."

Mel looked taken aback and, not for the

first time in her life, Lauren found herself wishing that Carla wasn't always so blunt.

"He's called that because when he was a foal he was almost black," Lauren explained. "That's right, isn't it, Mel?"

"Yeah." Mel nodded. "His coat got lighter as he got older, you see."

"It's still kind of weird," Carla said.

Mel frowned and for a moment she and Carla stared at each other in an unfriendly way. Lauren felt alarmed. She didn't want Carla and Mel to argue! To her relief, Anna changed the subject.

"So, do you two ride together a lot?" she asked Mel.

"Yes," Mel replied. "Most days after school and on the weekends we go out on the trails in the woods."

"The three of us went trail riding for a day last March," Carla said. "It was at a stable near my aunt's. It was great, wasn't it, Lauren?"

Lauren nodded. "Do you remember that water fight we had afterward?"

"When Anna sat in a bucket!" Carla said, grinning.

"I did not sit in a bucket. I was pushed!" Anna protested.

Mel spoke up. "We had lots of water fights *this* summer. Do you remember, Lauren, when —"

Carla interrupted her. "What about that hot-dog fight?" she said, speaking to Lauren. "In the evening when we were camping in my aunt's yard."

Lauren grinned. "Yeah. That was really funny." She turned to Mel. "The ketchup went all over the tent walls and Carla's aunt was pretty mad."

Carla and Anna giggled but Mel didn't look as if she found it that funny.

"It was a really great weekend," Carla went on. She started reminding the others about all the things they'd done together — the barbecue they'd had, the midnight feast, the canoe trip on the creek. . . .

"Lauren," Mel interrupted at last. "I'm going to go home."

Lauren was surprised. "But you haven't been here for long."

"I . . ." Mel hesitated. "I said I'd help my mom get lunch ready."

"Oh," Lauren said, feeling disappointed. "Well, Twilight's probably done enough for now. I'll ride him up the driveway with you to cool him off. Is that OK?" she said to Carla and Anna.

"Sure," they said.

She swapped with Carla and then she and Mel rode up the driveway.

"So?" Lauren asked eagerly. "What do you think of Carla and Anna?"

"Anna seems OK," Mel replied cautiously. "But Carla's a bit full of herself."

"That's just how she comes across at first," Lauren told her. "She's nice when you get to know her."

Mel raised her eyebrows as if she didn't believe her. "She's not a very good rider. She was pulling Twilight's mouth really hard."

"She wasn't pulling *really* hard," Lauren said in surprise. "And so what if she isn't a good rider? That's only because she hasn't had many lessons. She loves horses, and that's the main thing."

"Well, I wouldn't let her on Shadow," Mel declared.

"Twilight didn't mind," Lauren said defensively.

"I bet he did," Mel said.

"No, he didn't!"

Mel didn't reply and they rode the rest of the way in silence.

"See you, then," Lauren said when they reached the end of the driveway.

"Yeah, whatever," Mel muttered and, turning Shadow onto the road, she trotted away without looking back.

CHAPTER

Five

Lauren rode back to the farmhouse feeling confused. Why was Mel in such a bad mood? Trying to forget about it, she untacked Twilight, put him in his stable, and went into the house.

Her mom had made a delicious spaghetti bolognese for lunch. Afterward, Lauren, Carla, and Anna helped clear the table.

"What are you three going to do now?"

Mrs. Foster asked as they put the last of the plates in the dishwasher. "If you want, you could make some gingerbread decorations for the Christmas tree."

Lauren looked at her friends. "Well, I usually muck Twilight's stable out after lunch. How about we go do that first?"

"Muck his stable out?" Anna said. "What does that mean?"

"Take out the dirty straw," Lauren explained.

Carla frowned. "But it's raining."

Lauren glanced out the window. It was drizzling just slightly. "Only a little and we'll be inside the stable."

"Let's do it later," Carla said. "I'd like to make decorations."

Lauren gave in. "OK."

"You can decorate the shapes with white icing," Mrs. Foster said as she got out the pastry cutters. "Max, do you want to come help?"

It was great fun. Even Buddy tried to join in. He sat with his big nose right up to the tabletop, his dark eyes following them as they rolled and cut the gingerbread into stars, holly leaves, and candles.

"No, Buddy!" Lauren said quickly when she saw him licking his lips and eyeing a nearby star. "These aren't for you to eat." She cut out the last shape. "All finished," she declared. "Now they just need to cook."

After the gingerbread had cooked and

cooled down, they decorated it with white icing and silver sugar balls.

"OK, they need to dry now," Mrs. Foster said. "And then we can put some ribbon through them and hang them on the Christmas tree."

"Let's go and muck out," Lauren said to Carla and Anna.

Anna looked out the window at the gray skies. "It looks really cold."

"It won't be when we're in the stable," Lauren told her. "Come on!"

They pulled on their boots and coats and went outside.

Because Twilight's stable hadn't been mucked out earlier, his bed was messier than usual. Lauren got the wheelbarrow, three forks, a spade, and a brush. "I think we'd better muck him out really well so his bed will be nice and clean this evening," she told Carla and Anna.

Carla picked up a fork. "OK. What do we have to do?"

"The dirty straw goes in the wheelbarrow," Lauren explained. "And the clean straw goes against the wall of his stable. Like this." She showed them how to use a fork to shake the clean and dirty straw apart.

"Ew!" Anna said. "It smells terrible!"

Carla cautiously shook a forkful of straw. Some dirty straw fell on her glove. "Yuck!" she exclaimed, shaking it off.

Anna poked at a pile of straw with a fork. "I think this part is clean over here," she announced.

Carla giggled. "I'll do that part, then." She attempted to throw the clean straw into the pile against the wall but she picked up too much on her fork and it scattered all over the bed, mixing in with the droppings. "Whoops!" she said. "Sorry!"

Lauren began to think it would be much quicker to muck out on her own! "Look, maybe it would be best if I did this while you get some more clean straw," she suggested. "It's in the barn over there. Would you mind bringing me about five slices in a wheelbarrow?"

Carla and Anna nodded and went to the barn. They returned five minutes later with a laden wheelbarrow.

"Here we are!" Carla said cheerfully. "We've got the straw!"

Lauren looked at the barrow. "That's hay, not straw."

"Oh," Anna said, her face falling.

"Sorry, Lauren," Carla said.

"It doesn't matter," Lauren sighed. "I'll go get some more."

Looking as if they didn't really know what to do, Carla and Anna watched as she got some straw and spread it over the bed.

"Do you have to do this every day?" Anna asked.

Lauren nodded.

"Better you than me," Carla commented.

"Yeah," Anna agreed, shivering. "It's freezing out here!"

Lauren felt guilty. It was clear that neither Anna nor Carla were enjoying mucking out. She hurried through the chores. Soon the stable was finished, and Lauren brought Twilight in from the field.

"Night, boy," she said, rubbing Twilight's nose. *See you later on*, she thought.

Twilight looked at her, and Lauren was sure he was thinking the same thing.

"Come on, Lauren, let's go in!" Anna urged.

Lauren shut Twilight's door.

"So, what are we going to do tonight?" Carla said as they took their boots off in the porch. Her eyes lit up. "I know, why don't we have a midnight feast?"

"Yeah!" Anna said. "We brought lots of candy with us."

"OK," Lauren agreed. "But can we have it earlier than midnight? I have to get up to feed Twilight in the morning." *I wanted to take Twilight flying tonight, but I won't be able to if Carla and Anna are still awake!* she thought.

"But it won't be a midnight feast if we don't have it at midnight," Carla protested. "We can't have it earlier."

Lauren didn't want to seem like a spoilsport, and she really loved the idea of having a real midnight feast. She thought quickly. She was sure Twilight wouldn't mind if she missed flying that night. "OK, midnight's fine," she agreed.

"Cool!" Anna said.

"So what candy do you have?" Lauren asked.

"All kinds," Carla told her. "Let's go to your room and we'll show you."

"OK," Lauren agreed happily, and they all hurried upstairs.

CHAPTER

Six

When Lauren's alarm clock went off the next morning, she felt so tired that she could hardly drag herself out of bed. She and Carla and Anna had stayed awake talking and eating candy until almost two o'clock in the morning.

"What time is it?" Carla murmured sleepily as Lauren tried to find her jeans.

"Quarter to seven. I've got to feed Twilight." Lauren yawned.

"What, now?" Carla said. "Go back to bed. He won't mind waiting."

But, tired as she was, Lauren knew there was no way she could go back to bed knowing Twilight was waiting for his breakfast.

Leaving Carla and Anna to go back to sleep, she went downstairs. A heavy frost had fallen in the night — so heavy that Lauren left footprints in it as she trudged down the path to Twilight's stable. He whinnied when he saw her.

"I'm really sorry I didn't come out last night," she told him, going into the stable and putting her arms around his neck.

"Carla and Anna wanted to have a midnight feast." She bit her lip. "Actually, I think it's going to be too risky to try to come flying while they're sharing a room with me. What if they wake up and find I'm gone?"

Twilight stared at her.

Lauren wished she could turn him into a unicorn so she could really talk to him. "I don't know what to do," she told him. "I know you love flying but I just don't know if I should risk it."

Twilight lifted his muzzle to her face and blew out gently.

"Are you trying to say it's OK?" Lauren asked.

Twilight nodded.

Lauren rested her forehead
against his. "Thanks,
Twilight. We'll be able
to go flying again
soon. I promise."

Twilight stamped his hoof. Lauren took
the hint. "All right. You're hungry. I'll go
get your breakfast."

Fifteen minutes later, leaving Twilight
with some fresh water and a big haynet to
munch, Lauren went back to the house. It
was almost nine o'clock before Carla and
Anna got up.

"I can't believe you have to get up so
early every day, even during the holidays."
Carla yawned as she pulled on her clothes.

"You used to hate getting up early," Anna said.

Lauren shrugged. "It's just one of those things you have to do when you've got a pony."

After breakfast they went outside. Remembering the day before, Lauren decided it might be easier if Carla and Anna groomed Twilight while she mucked out. That way they didn't have to get dirty.

"We don't mind helping you muck out," Anna said when Lauren told them her plan.

"Really," Carla said. "It was fun yesterday."

"It's OK," Lauren replied hastily, sure

that they were only offering because they were being polite. "It'll be quicker if I do it. At least I know the difference between hay and straw," she tried to joke.

Unfortunately, Carla and Anna didn't seem to think it was funny. They both looked quite hurt.

"We didn't mean to get it wrong yesterday," Carla said.

"We just didn't know," Anna put in.

"Yeah, we're not all lucky enough to have ponies of our own," Carla said.

"I know. I'm sorry," Lauren apologized. "I didn't mean it like that."

"Are you sure you can *trust* us to groom Twilight?" Carla said sarcastically.

"Of course I can," Lauren said. "And

you can help me muck out if you really want to."

"No, no, it's obvious we don't know enough," Carla retorted.

Lauren knew that when Carla was in this kind of mood it was best just to ignore her. So, giving Anna and Carla the grooming kit, she started to muck out. Luckily by the time they took Twilight into the field, Carla's bad mood seemed to have lifted.

They took turns riding Twilight. Anna was still nervous but Carla was growing in confidence. She cantered Twilight twice around the field and although she lost her stirrup and had to hang on to his mane, she seemed delighted to have gone so fast.

"Can I try jumping him?" she asked eagerly.

Lauren hesitated. She knew the only reason Carla had stayed on was because Twilight was being so well-behaved. "Maybe tomorrow. Twilight's done enough today."

"OK," Carla agreed reluctantly.

They untacked Twilight and went inside.

Lauren's dad was making a cup of coffee. "Lauren, Mel called while you were with Twilight. She asked if you would call her back."

Lauren nodded. She was about to pick up the phone when she remembered the bad mood Mel had been in the day before. Maybe she'd call her later, she decided.

"So what are we going to do now?" Carla asked.

"I don't know," Lauren answered. "We could play with my model horses or read pony magazines." She and Mel often did things like that when they were inside. But neither Anna nor Carla looked that eager.

"Couldn't we go out or something?" Carla suggested.

Just then, Mr. Foster spoke. "How about we take a trip into town? There's a Christmas market being held on the main street today."

"That sounds cool!" Carla said.

Anna nodded. "I brought some money with me. I can buy some presents to take home."

"Me, too," Carla put in.

"OK," Lauren said. "We'd like to go, Dad."

"Sure," Mr. Foster said. "I'll go tell your mom and Max while you three get your coats."

Half an hour later, Mr. Foster parked the car on a side street in town. Lauren piled out with Carla, Anna, and Max. The cold air was filled with the smell of roasting chestnuts. "Doesn't it smell Christmassy!" Lauren exclaimed.

"Yeah. Where are the booths?" Carla asked, looking around.

"On the main street," Mrs. Foster said. "It's this way."

They headed into the town center.
There were people everywhere, bustling
along with bags and shopping baskets, and
Christmas music was playing in every store
they passed. Lauren felt happiness bubbling
inside her. Christmas suddenly felt very
close!

"Brr, it's cold," Anna said, pulling her
coat around her.

"At least it's not raining," Mrs. Foster said.

But she spoke too soon. Just then, a
raindrop spattered against Lauren's sleeve.

"Maybe I shouldn't have said anything,"
Mrs. Foster said ruefully. "Hopefully, it's
just a passing shower. Come on, let's
hurry!"

To everyone's relief, by the time they

reached the main street the rain had
stopped. A very Christmassy scene greeted
them. There were about thirty booths
selling everything from wreaths to
homemade stockings. A group of
Christmas carolers were singing near a
small platform, and a man was roasting
chestnuts nearby. Lauren looked around
excitedly. There were so many things
to see.

Max pointed to the end of the street
where a large Christmas tree was towering
up into the sky. It was decorated with silver
and gold lights. "Wow! Look at that
Christmas tree! It's huge!"

Carla looked at it and shrugged. "That's
nothing compared to the one we've got

back home. It's about twice as tall and it's
got lots more lights on it, doesn't it, Anna?"

Anna nodded. "Yeah, it's much bigger."
She looked around. "There aren't many
booths, are there? I thought it would be a
really big market."

She sounded disappointed, and Lauren felt her excitement dampen slightly. Her friends didn't seem very impressed with the market.

"Well, I'm sure you'll find some things you want to buy," Mrs. Foster told them. "Now, why don't you three go look around on your own? We'll meet you by the Christmas tree in forty minutes. Then we can get some hot cider and Christmas cookies."

Lauren, Anna, and Carla set off. To Lauren's relief, her friends seemed to cheer up as they started to look at the different things.

"Look at these!" Anna said, dragging Lauren over to look at a booth that was selling beautifully iced gingerbread houses. "I bet my mom would like one. She loves gingerbread and these are really pretty."

"And there's a place over there selling salt-dough decorations," Carla said. "My grandmother loves those. I could buy her something to put on her Christmas tree."

Lauren had her eye on a booth that was selling homemade candy. "I want to go over there," she said. "Those candies look delicious!"

It didn't take them long at all to spend their money!

"What should we do now?" Carla asked. She looked at her watch. "We're not meeting your mom and dad for another ten minutes."

Just then, it started to rain again.

"Let's go wait over there," Lauren said, pointing to a store doorway near the Christmas tree. "At least we'll be out of the rain." The others nodded but by the time they reached the doorway, it was already full of other people who had the same idea.

The three girls stood against the wall of the building. It sheltered them slightly from the rain but not from the cold.

"I'm freezing." Carla shivered.

"Me, too!" Anna agreed. "I hope your mom and dad come soon, Lauren."

Lauren hoped so, too. Her hands and feet were cold, and now that the excitement of shopping was over, she felt suddenly tired. Her late-night and early-morning start were catching up with her.

It began to rain more heavily. "This is awful," Carla complained as raindrops splashed on her coat.

"I want to go back to the farm," Anna said. She and Carla huddled together.

Lauren scanned the street. Where were her mom and dad and Max? *Come on,* she thought, looking guiltily at her unhappy friends. *Please hurry up!*

Just then, her dad came hurrying through the crowd. He had a large umbrella with him.

"Dad!" Lauren called in relief.

Mr. Foster came hurrying over. "There you are!" he said. "Get under here before you get any wetter."

The three girls quickly joined him. "Where are Mom and Max?" Lauren asked.

"They went back to the car," Mr. Foster replied. "It looks like we're going to have to abandon this shopping trip, I'm afraid."

Anna nodded. "I'm really cold."

"Come on, then," Mr. Foster said. "Let's go home."

★　★　★

It was a relief to get back into the car. Mrs. Foster had the engine running and the heater on.

"Well, that was a bit of a washout," she said, looking over her shoulder as they set off for the farm. "Sorry about that, girls."

"It's OK," Carla said, looking happier now that she was in the warm car. "At least we got some shopping done."

"Yeah, I bought a gingerbread house for my mom, and some candy," Anna put in.

"And it was fun until it started raining," Carla said.

Despite her friends' upbeat words, Lauren couldn't help still feeling guilty. She was sure they hadn't really enjoyed the market. She bit her lip. Carla and Anna's stay wasn't turning out like she'd expected at all. She'd wanted them to have a really good time while they were staying with her but everything just kept going wrong.

Carla turned to her. "What are we going to do tomorrow, Lauren?"

"I don't know," Lauren replied in a subdued voice.

"Well, what do you normally do during the holidays and weekends?" Anna asked.

Lauren shrugged. "Do things with Twilight — go for rides in the woods."

Carla frowned. "That sounds kind of boring."

"It isn't," Lauren protested. "The woods are great." As she spoke, she had an idea.

Why didn't she take Carla and Anna to the secret clearing? It was an amazing place even if she couldn't tell them it was magic. "There's lots to see in the woods. Like this clearing I know that's down a hidden path. It's got pink rocks all around it and these amazing purple flowers all over the grass even in winter."

"Really?" said Anna, looking interested.

Lauren nodded. "In the evening there are hundreds of fireflies and in the summer there are butterflies everywhere."

"It sounds cool!" said Carla. "Can we go?"

"Well, it's a very difficult ride. . . ." Lauren began. As Carla began to frown, she hastily added, "But I'm sure you'll be able to manage it. We can go tomorrow, if you want."

Carla and Anna nodded eagerly.

As Lauren watched the houses flashing past, she thought about taking Anna and Carla to the clearing. No one knew about it — not even Mel. She felt a flicker of nervousness. She just hoped Carla and Anna liked it enough to see that staying in the country with her really was fun after all.

CHAPTER

Seven

When Lauren came in from feeding Twilight the following morning, the phone was ringing. It was Jessica.

"Hi, Lauren. I . . . um . . . well, I was just wondering if you were still coming over to Mel's this morning." Jessica sounded uncomfortable.

"To Mel's?" Lauren frowned.

"To practice for the show. We arranged it last week."

Lauren's eyes widened. She'd completely forgotten that they'd agreed to have a practice that day.

"Mel said she called yesterday to remind you but you didn't call her back." Jessica hesitated. "I . . . I think she's a little upset, Lauren."

Lauren felt guilty. She'd been so busy with Carla and Anna that Mel's phone message had slipped her mind. "It was just a mistake," she said quickly.

"Well, are you coming today?" Jess asked.

Lauren felt torn. What about Carla and Anna? They were expecting to go to the secret glade in the woods. "I don't know. It's difficult because of Carla and Anna but I'll try my best to come."

"OK," Jessica said slowly. "Well, I guess I might see you later."

Lauren put the phone down. What was she going to do?

Mrs. Foster came into the kitchen. "Is everything OK?" she asked, seeing Lauren's worried face.

Sitting down at the kitchen table, Lauren told her about the mix-up.

"Well, can't Carla and Anna go to Mel's with you?" her mom asked.

"I don't think Mel likes Carla very much," Lauren said, and she told her mom about Mel's bad mood on Saturday.

Mrs. Foster sighed. "Oh, dear. I see."

"What should I do, Mom?" Lauren asked.

"I think you should probably go to Mel's house," Mrs. Foster replied. "It sounds to me as if Mel might be feeling a little left out because of you having Carla and Anna here, and I'm sure they won't mind if you're only gone for a few hours. Wait till they wake up and then see what they say."

Carla and Anna seemed a bit surprised when they came downstairs and Lauren said she had to go over to Mel's to practice for the show.

"But you said we could go to that clearing in the woods!" Carla protested.

"I'm really sorry," Lauren told her. "I'd forgotten all about this practice. We're doing all sorts of pony races on Wednesday — sack race, egg and spoon —"

"Can we come watch you practice?" Anna asked.

"Yeah, it sounds fun," Carla agreed. "We could help you set everything out."

Lauren felt alarmed. How would Mel react if she brought Carla and Anna? Lauren was sure she wouldn't be too happy. "You wouldn't know what to do," she said quickly.

"Well, you could tell us," Carla replied.

"It'll just waste time if we have to stop and explain everything," Lauren told her.

Carla frowned. "It can't be that hard."

To Lauren's relief, her mom spoke. "I think it might be best if you stay here, Carla. It's so cold today. You'll freeze if you're standing around waiting to have a ride. Why don't you and Anna stay and help me ice the Christmas cake instead?"

"I love icing Christmas cakes," Anna said.

Carla hesitated. "OK, we'll stay," she agreed, shooting Lauren an annoyed look.

Lauren sighed. She seemed to be annoying *all* her friends at the moment!

Riding up the driveway to Mel's house later that morning, Lauren felt nervous. What sort of mood would Mel be in? She was obviously fed up that Lauren hadn't called her back the day before.

"Hi," Lauren called as she rode over to the field gate.

Mel and Jessica were cantering around the field on Shadow and Sandy. They slowed down and rode over to meet her.

Jessica smiled. "Hi, Lauren."

Mel didn't say anything.

Lauren felt awful. She'd never fallen out with Mel before and she didn't like it.

"Sorry I didn't call you back yesterday, Mel."

"Yeah, well, I guess you forgot," Mel said coldly.

"It's just that we all went out and —" Lauren stammered.

"Whatever," Mel interrupted. "It doesn't matter."

There was a moment's silence.

"Well, should we start to practice, then?" Jessica said quickly. "How about we start with a bending race?"

"Great," Lauren said. "But I can't stay too long. I've got to get back to —"

"Carla and Anna," Mel finished. "You don't have to be here at all if you don't want to be, Lauren."

"I *do* want to be here!" Lauren protested.

Mel raised her eyebrows. Lauren felt herself starting to get annoyed. She'd said she was sorry about not calling her. What else could she do? She frowned and opened her mouth but before she could say anything, Jessica spoke up. "Come on, let's start!"

Lauren kept quiet.

They rode over to where there were three buckets and, a little way off, three barrels with a pile of potatoes on top.

"We have to gallop up and get a potato, then gallop back and throw it into the bucket," Jessica said. "Ready, steady, go!"

The three ponies surged forward but Lauren's mind wasn't on the games and it seemed like Mel's wasn't, either. Both of them missed the bucket and Jessica was easily the winner.

The sack race was no better. Shadow galloped straight past the sack, and Lauren fell over.

The other races went just as badly. The final straw came when Lauren tripped over Twilight's legs in the walk, gallop, and lead, making Shadow pull back in alarm. Mel lost her grip on his reins and he trotted off around the field, refusing to be caught for ten minutes.

When Mel finally did catch him, Jessica looked at her and Lauren in exasperation. "We're going to do terribly on Wednesday if we're as bad as this."

"Well, maybe if Lauren could stop falling over, it would help." Mel frowned.

"And maybe if you could hang on to your reins, then we wouldn't have to spend so much time catching Shadow," Lauren retorted. She was freezing cold from standing around and totally fed up. She'd upset Carla already by coming over. The

last thing she needed was Mel snapping at her, too. "I'm going home," she said.

"But Lauren, what about practicing?" Jessica protested.

"It's too cold," Lauren said. "I'll see you on Wednesday." And before Jessica could say anything more, she turned and rode Twilight away.

As she rode him along the road, she felt her anger die down. She shouldn't really have left like that but she'd been feeling so fed up with Mel.

"Oh, Twilight." She sighed, stroking his neck. "What am I going to do?" More than anything, she wanted to turn him into a unicorn.

She saw a dense grove of trees at the edge of the road and decided to risk it. Riding him into the trees, she checked that there was no one around and said the magic spell. With a flash, Twilight turned into a unicorn.

Lauren hugged him.

"You're not having a good day, are you?" he said, nuzzling her.

"No," she replied. "Everyone's annoyed with me, Twilight. The practice was awful. I don't know what to do."

"Me, neither," Twilight admitted. "I don't think they're the kind of problems my magic can solve."

Lauren leaned her head against his neck.

Just talking to him had made her feel
better. "I should turn you back," she said
reluctantly. "Someone might come along."

Twilight nodded. "Things will get
better, Lauren. I'm sure they will."

Lauren hoped he was right. Saying the Undoing Spell, she turned him back into a pony.

"Come on," she said with a sigh. "Let's go home."

CHAPTER

Eight

"Hi," Lauren called, going into the kitchen. Carla and Anna were just cleaning up after icing the Christmas cake. "The cake looks great," Lauren said, admiring the huge cake with crisp snowy peaks of white icing. It was decorated with plastic robins and snowmen.

"Thanks," Anna said. "We helped your mom make some muffins, too," she said, pointing to a tray of sweet-smelling muffins on the side. "How was your practice?"

"Oh, OK," said Lauren, not wanting to talk about it. She glanced at Carla, who was screwing the lid on the jar of icing. "I'm sorry I had to go off like that," she apologized. "What would you like to do this afternoon? We can do anything you like."

Carla looked up. "Can we ride Twilight in the woods?"

"Yes, can we go to that clearing?" Anna asked. "The one you told us about?"

"Sure," Lauren agreed. "We'll go this afternoon."

★ ★ ★

But when they went outside to Twilight's field after lunch, the clouds overhead looked heavy and the air seemed strangely still and quiet.

"I think it's going to snow," Lauren said, her breath coming out in a cloud. "We'd better not go to the woods, after all."

"Why not?" said Carla.

"It'll be too dangerous if it snows," Lauren explained. "The paths will get slippery and if there's a blizzard, we might get lost."

Carla looked at the sky. "It's not going to snow. It's just cold, that's all. Come on, let's go."

"No," Lauren said. "It's too dangerous."

Carla frowned. "I bet you're just saying it's going to snow because you think we're not good enough to go riding in the woods."

"Of course I don't think that —" Lauren started to protest but just then her dad drove up in his Land Rover, with the livestock trailer bumping along behind.

"Lauren!" he called. "Are you free? I

have to go to the East Hill field and bring
in the four ewes who are about to lamb. I
don't want them cut off on the hillside if it
starts to snow. Do you think you could
come help me?"

"Of course," Lauren said. She looked
uncertainly at the others.

"It's OK, we can ride later," Anna said.
"Come on, let's go help your dad."

Lauren thought for a moment. The East
Hill field was really muddy and cold. She
was sure Carla and Anna would hate it.
"You don't have to come. You could stay
and ride in Twilight's field. I don't mind
going with Dad on my own."

"But we might be able to help," Carla
said.

Lauren remembered the last time she had helped her dad round up sheep. She had ended up splattered in mud from head to toe. "No, really," she insisted. "You stay. Dad and I will manage fine."

"But it'll be easier with four of us," Carla pointed out.

"You won't know what to do," Lauren said as her dad beeped his horn.

"Lauren, we're not totally useless, you know," Carla said, sounding exasperated.

Mr. Foster beeped his horn again. "Look, don't worry about it," Lauren said hastily, and she hurried over to the gate.

As she got into the Land Rover, she glanced back. Carla and Anna both looked upset and angry. Lauren's heart sank. She'd meant to save them from doing something they wouldn't enjoy but it just looked like she'd hurt their feelings. She pushed her hands through her hair. She'd never thought having her friends stay over would be so stressful!

As Lauren helped her dad round up the sheep and put them in the back of the Land Rover, she thought about Carla and Anna. She hoped they were having a good time riding Twilight.

It was cold on the hillside and as Mr. Foster caught the last sheep, it started to snow.

Within minutes, the flakes were falling thick and fast.

"Looks like we got here just in time," said her dad. He nudged the sheep up the ramp of the trailer. "Come on, let's get back to the farm."

As they bumped down the rough track, Lauren watched the fields turning white. She hoped Carla and Anna had

remembered to untack Twilight and put
his rug on.

Mr. Foster stopped the Land Rover
by Twilight's stable. "You get the others
and hurry into the house," he said. "I'll
just drop the ewes off in the lower
paddock."

Lauren nodded and got out. Her dad
drove off and she went to Twilight's stable.
She looked over the door. "Hi." She
stopped. The stable was empty!

She searched around. Where were Carla
and Anna? Where was Twilight?

She hurried to the tack room. There
was no sign of her friends but there was a
note on the table.

Dear Lauren

 We're bored of riding in the field so we're going to the woods. Don't worry! We're not totally useless. We'll be fine.

Lots of love,
Carla and Anna xxx

Lauren stared at the note. Carla and Anna had gone into the woods, even though she had told them not to! What if they couldn't find the way home in the snow, or Twilight slipped and hurt himself? They'd be stuck outside in the freezing cold. Lauren's heart pounded.

 What was she going to do?

CHAPTER

Nine

Lauren stood in the doorway to the tack room. The snow was falling thick and fast now. Her dad was down in the lower pastures with the sheep and her mom was in town with Max. She didn't even have Twilight.

I've got to go after them, she thought. *I need to make sure they're OK.*

Even as she thought it, she realized it

would be stupid to go into the woods on
her own. But who could go with her?

Mel.

Pushing all thoughts of their argument
to the back of her mind, Lauren ran to the
farmhouse. Mel might be irritated with her
but this was an emergency.

Stumbling into the kitchen, she grabbed
the phone and punched in Mel's number.

"Hello?" Mel answered.

"Mel, it's me," Lauren said urgently.

"Oh, hi." Mel's voice was cold, and
Lauren felt a sudden flicker of doubt. What
if Mel was so annoyed with her that she
refused to help?

"Carla and Anna have taken Twilight
into the woods," Lauren blurted out, her

heart beating wildly as she wondered how she was going to persuade Mel to help. "I'm going to have to go after them and help them get home safely. There's no one else here and well, I —"

"Do you want me to help?" Mel interrupted her, the frostiness vanishing instantly from her voice. "I'll come over right away and we can go together. I'll bring Shadow and Sandy. It'll be much faster if we go on horseback."

Relief rushed through Lauren. "Oh, thank you. Thank you so much!"

"Get a flashlight and a thermos of hot chocolate," Mel instructed. "And write your dad a note so he knows where we've gone. I'll see you in a minute!"

Lauren quickly did as Mel had said. While the kettle boiled, she wrote a note saying they'd gone into the woods and then she found a flashlight and shoved it into a backpack. She also added a blanket and a couple of extra scarves.

She was filling the flask when she heard a knock on the window. Mel was outside with Shadow and Sandy. Grabbing the bag, Lauren hurried outside.

"I've got some granola bars, mittens, and a first-aid kit," Mel told her. "I called Jessica and she said it's fine to take Sandy." She threw Sandy's reins to Lauren. "Come on! Let's go!"

Lauren scrambled onto the palomino's back, and they cantered down the path.

"How long have they been gone?" Mel shouted through the swirling snow.

"About half an hour, I think," Lauren replied breathlessly, screwing up her eyes against the stinging snowflakes. "But they might have been gone longer." She explained about leaving them with Twilight while she went to help her dad.

"Which way do you think they would have gone?" Mel asked, reining Shadow in as they came to a fork in the path.

"I bet they took the main trail," Lauren said. She wished she had Twilight. He would have understood that they were trying to find Carla and Anna and would have helped them follow their tracks.

They trotted down the left-hand fork. Sandy's hooves slipped and the young pony stopped uncertainly. "Come on, boy. It's OK," Lauren said.

She could tell Sandy didn't like the icy ground. "We'd better just take it slowly," she called to Mel.

They walked on, the ponies' hooves sliding every now and then in the snow. Lauren's fingers and toes got colder and colder despite her gloves and thick socks.

"What if they didn't come this way?" Mel said after a while.

"They must have. They wouldn't have

gone down the narrow trail," Lauren
pointed out.

"They might," Mel said.

They halted the ponies and looked at
each other uncertainly.

"What should we do?" Lauren asked.

"Maybe we should turn around," Mel
suggested.

Lauren was about to agree when all
of a sudden, her eyes caught sight of
four long silvery hairs caught on a
bramble that was sticking out into the
path. "Look!" she exclaimed. "They
look like hairs from Twilight's tail!
They must have come this way." She
rode over and pulled the hairs off the
bramble.

"We don't know they're Twilight's,"
Mel said uncertainly. "They could be any
gray pony's."

"No," Lauren said, shaking her head
and looking at the hairs in her gloved
hand. "I'm sure they're Twilight's. We've
got to keep going, Mel!"

To her relief, Mel didn't argue. "OK,"
she said. "Come on."

They rode on and Lauren scanned the
trail ahead. It was hard to see through the
swirling snowflakes. Sandy's head drooped
and she edged nearer to Shadow's side.
Patting her neck to encourage her,
Lauren felt a flicker of despair. How
were they ever going to find Twilight,
Carla, and Anna? The woods were so
deep and vast. Twilight could be
anywhere — down a dead-end trail, near
the quarry. . . .

Just then, a tree loomed up out of the
snow in front of them. Sandy stopped with
a snort.

"We've ridden off the main trail," Mel

said. She looked around. Her face was worried. "If we're not careful, we're going to get lost, Lauren. I really think we should go back and get help."

Lauren hesitated.

"Come on," Mel urged. "We can't risk getting stuck out here ourselves."

Part of Lauren knew Mel was right but she couldn't bear to turn around. Her friends could be in real trouble. She put her hands to her mouth. "Twilight!" she shouted desperately. "Carla! Anna!"

Shadow lifted his head and whinnied, too.

There was a moment's silence. Lauren's heart sank. They were going to have to turn around. Mel was right. If they got lost, then there would be no one to get help. . . .

Suddenly, her thoughts were interrupted by a faint answering neigh.

Lauren would have known that sound anywhere. "Twilight!" She gasped. "Come on, Mel! He's nearby!"

They headed in the direction of the whinny, weaving in and out of the snow-covered trees, their eyes peering through the blizzard.

"Twilight!" Lauren shouted again.

There was another answering whinny and suddenly, just down the trail, Lauren saw Carla and Anna and Twilight sheltering under the branches of a huge fir tree.

"Lauren!" Anna shouted. "We're over here!"

Lauren touched her heels to Sandy's sides and trotted over. Carla was holding her wrist.

"Are you OK?" Lauren asked, jumping off.

"I hurt my wrist." Carla was shivering. "Oh, Lauren, I'm so glad to see you."

"We didn't know what to do," Anna said. "Carla's wrist was hurting so much she couldn't get back on Twilight to ride home. I was going to come for help but I thought I might get lost and Carla didn't want me to leave her on her own."

"What happened?" Mel demanded.

"It started to snow, and Twilight didn't seem to want to go any farther," Anna explained, her voice trembling. "Carla was riding him and he just kept stopping."

"I tried to make him go on," Carla said. "But he threw his head in the air so I got off to lead him. I was trying to lead him along the path when I slipped on some ice

and fell and hurt my wrist." She looked
like she was about to cry. "I'm really sorry,
Lauren."

"It doesn't matter," Lauren said.

"You look freezing," Mel said to Carla.
"Here, we've got some hot chocolate and
some mittens." She dismounted and started
pulling things out of her backpack.

"I'll go for help on Twilight," Lauren
said, shrugging off her own backpack and
handing it to Mel.

Mel nodded. "Good idea. I'll stay with
Carla and Anna."

"Oh, thank you, Mel!" Carla burst out.

"Do you mind staying?" Anna asked her.

"Not at all," Mel answered. She looked
at Lauren. "Go on!"

Jumping onto Twilight, Lauren turned
and they made their way carefully through
the trees. Carla and Anna were both
looking really pale and cold and she knew
she had to get help quickly. As soon as she
was out of sight of the others, she
dismounted and said the Turning Spell.

In a flash, Twilight was a unicorn. "I'm
sorry, Lauren," he blurted out. "I tried to
get them to turn back but they just kept
making me go on."

"It's OK," Lauren said. "Come on, let's
go get my dad. It will be quicker if we fly."

Twilight nodded and she got back on.
He flew up into the treetops. The snow
was falling faster than ever and Lauren
could hardly see through it.

A tree loomed up out of the snow. "Look out!" Lauren cried.

Twilight swerved just in time. "Sorry." He gasped. "I can't see very well."

He weaved in and out of the trees. Lauren clung on tightly. It was a very uncomfortable ride. Snowflakes hit her face, catching on her eyelashes and blinding her. Her skin felt numb with cold. She remembered what Mrs. Fontana had said about flying through the snow. *"It'll be a wonderful experience,"* the bookstore owner had told her. *"You won't forget it."*

Mrs. Fontana must be crazy, Lauren thought. *This isn't wonderful at all. It's dreadful!*

Twilight changed direction and then changed direction again. He slowed down uncertainly.

"What are you doing?" Lauren demanded. "Come on, Twilight. Fly faster! We've got to get help."

"I'm not sure where we are," Twilight replied. He shook his head. "I . . . I think we're lost."

"Lost!" Lauren echoed. "We can't be!"

"But I really don't know where we are," Twilight said, flying down to the forest floor.

Frustration welled up inside Lauren. This couldn't be happening. Carla and Anna needed her to get home, to get help. "For goodness' sake, Twilight!" she cried.

"You're a unicorn! You're supposed to have magic powers. How come you can't even fly through a snowstorm?"

"I'm sorry, but I just don't know how," Twilight said unhappily.

Lauren thought of her friends in the cold and lost her temper. "This is so stupid!" she shouted.

"Lauren!" Twilight protested, stamping a front hoof in the snow.

At once a purple spark flew up from the snow and hovered in front of his nose. Twilight snorted in surprise.

"What's that?" Lauren said, astonishment making her forget her anger.

"I don't know." Twilight peered at the spark. The air around it was shimmering in

a pale violet circle that got bigger and bigger as they watched. "It feels warm."

Lauren's eyes opened wide. "Look at the snow around it!"

As the snowflakes touched the edge of the violet they vanished so that there was no snow falling inside the circle.

Lauren and Twilight stared. What was going on?

CHAPTER

Ten

The purple spark is melting the snow!"
Twilight exclaimed.

"It must be one of your secret unicorn
powers," Lauren said. "Quick, stamp your
hoof again."

Twilight stamped his hoof in the snow
and another spark flew up. It hovered over
his ears, and instantly snow stopped falling
on his head.

Twilight stamped again and again. Soon there was a whole line of sparks arching over him and Lauren. Their shimmering violet glow melted the snowflakes so that they could see ahead, and kept them dry and warm inside the circle.

"Oh, Twilight!" Lauren gasped. "This is fantastic. Now we'll be able to find our way home."

Twilight plunged into the air. The late-afternoon sky was dark now, but the arch shimmered above him like a rainbow. Lauren felt warmth flow through her as they cantered through the sky. It was amazing to be able to canter through the falling snow without it touching them.

She looked up and saw the magic

rainbow arching overhead, a mass of glittering, shiny sparks. Her skin seemed to tingle and glow. It was like being in a magic bubble, just her and Twilight, separated from the world. She stroked his smooth, warm neck and watched the snow flash by.

"I know where we are," Twilight said suddenly. "We're not far from home. Hold on tight!"

Lauren gasped in delight as he swooped through the snow so fast that the winter sky blurred lilac around her. The wind streamed through her hair and she laughed out loud. Suddenly, she understood what Mrs. Fontana had meant about flying in the snow. She knew she would never forget this. Not ever!

In less than five minutes, they were at the edge of the woods. Twilight flew to the ground, and Lauren quickly turned him back into a pony. They galloped out of the trees and up the path.

Her dad was hurrying out of the house,

the keys of the Land Rover in his hand. Lauren guessed he had seen her note.

"Dad!" she shouted. "Carla and Anna are in the woods. Carla has hurt herself! Quick! They need help!"

It didn't take her long to explain what had happened. Mr. Foster got into the Land Rover and followed her into the woods. Surefooted as ever, Twilight cantered along the track until they reached the tree where Carla's, Anna, and Mel were sheltering.

Lauren was relieved to see that some color had come back into Carla's and Anna's cheeks. Mel had made them wrap blankets around their shoulders and shared the hot chocolate and granola bars. With

mittens to keep their hands warm and the
spare scarves around their necks, they
looked much more cheerful. Mel had even
put a bandage from the first-aid kit on
Carla's injured wrist.

"Mel's been fantastic!" Carla called to
Lauren as she reined Twilight to a halt
beside them.

"Absolutely great!" Anna agreed. "It
would have been awful staying in the
woods on our own."

"You've done a great job, Mel," Mr.
Foster said. "Well done."

Mel smiled. "No problem. I was just
glad I could help."

Lauren beamed at her, hoping her
friend could tell how grateful she was.

"Come on," Mr. Foster said to Carla and Anna. "Let's get you back to the farmhouse." He gently helped Carla to her feet.

Carla looked at Lauren. "I . . . I'm really sorry we brought Twilight out into the woods and caused so many problems, Lauren."

"It's OK," Lauren told her as she got into the car.

"We wanted to prove to you we weren't useless," Anna said. She bit her lip. "I guess we didn't do that."

Lauren frowned. "But I don't think you're useless."

"You do," Carla said. "You won't even let us muck out."

"But you don't like it," Lauren said. "You kept going on about how dirty and smelly and cold it was."

"We don't really mind it," Anna said. "It was just a bit of a surprise at first."

"And you were worried about getting mud on your jeans," Lauren reminded Carla.

"Only my new jeans," Carla told her. "I don't mind getting my old jeans dirty."

"Oh," said Lauren.

Mr. Foster looked at them. "It sounds like there's been a little misunderstanding."

"We've just been feeling really dumb," Carla said. "At least compared to you, Lauren."

Anna nodded. "You know so much now about horses and the countryside. We thought you might not want to be our friend anymore."

Lauren swallowed. "I guess I do know different stuff now," she admitted. "But you're still my friends." She looked at them. "And you'll always be my friends."

The two girls looked very happy.

"Really?" Carla said.

"Really!" Lauren promised, amazed they could have thought otherwise.

The next minute they were all hugging.

"Ow!" Carla gasped as her wrist knocked into Lauren's back.

"Come on," said Mr. Foster. "I think it's time we went home. Lauren, will you and Mel bring the ponies back?"

Lauren nodded.

Mr. Foster started the Land Rover and drove slowly away. Carla and Anna waved out of the back window until they vanished around a bend in the trail.

Lauren and Mel got back on Twilight and Shadow and, with Mel leading Sandy, they set off through the trees.

Lauren glanced at her friend. "Thanks for helping, Mel," she said quietly.

"That's OK," Mel replied. "I'm relieved that they were both all right — and Twilight, too, of course."

Lauren felt a rush of gratitude. "I'm sorry we argued, Mel," she said impulsively. "I really did mean to call you back yesterday, I just forgot."

"I shouldn't have made such a big deal out of it." Mel sighed. "I guess I was just feeling a little jealous. It was weird seeing you with other friends — other best friends." She looked down at Shadow's mane.

Lauren hesitated. "Carla and Anna are my best old friends and I still really like them, but you and Jess are just as

important. You're my best *new* friends."
She looked at Mel. "Is that OK?"

To her delight, Mel looked happy.
"Yes," she said. "It is."

They smiled and rode on.

"Well, I guess you'll be busy with Carla
and Anna tomorrow," Mel said when they
reached her house. "So I'll see you on
Christmas Eve."

Lauren had a sudden idea. "Or you and
Jessica could come over to my house
tomorrow," she suggested. "If the weather's
better, I'm going to take Carla and Anna
to this secret clearing I found in the
woods. We could all go together and then
in the afternoon we could get the ponies
ready for the show."

"OK," Mel said. "I'll see you tomorrow, then." She clicked her tongue and rode Shadow toward the fields. "You know," she said, looking around and grinning, "maybe Carla isn't that bad after all."

Lauren grinned back. "See you tomorrow!" she said, and she rode away down the driveway.

The snow had stopped now and as she rode through the silent white world, Lauren finally understood what Mrs. Fontana had meant about all friends being important — old friends, new friends, and special friends. She wanted — and needed — them all. Suddenly, Lauren realized she had one more apology to make.

She turned Twilight into the grove of trees at the side of the road and said the words of the Turning Spell.

With a flash, Twilight turned into a unicorn. "Oh, Twilight," Lauren said. "I'm really sorry I lost my temper in the snow. I wasn't really angry with you."

"It's OK," Twilight told her. "You were just worried about your friends. And now we've discovered how much fun flying in the snow can be!" He blew on her hands. "It hasn't been an easy week for you, Lauren."

Lauren's heart swelled. She'd hardly had any time to spend with Twilight over the last few days but he had never once gotten annoyed or upset with her. "I love you," she told him, stroking his mane. "I've hardly had any time for you but you've never stopped being my friend."

"I couldn't," Twilight said simply. He nuzzled her. "I'm your unicorn, Lauren. That means we're friends forever."

Lauren's eyes prickled with happy tears. "Forever," she whispered, hugging him.

CHAPTER

Eleven

The next morning dawned without a cloud to be seen in the bright blue sky. The snow sparkled like diamonds in the gentle winter sun. Mel and Jessica came over at ten o'clock and the five girls set off to the clearing. On the way there, they kept trading places so everyone got to ride. Even Carla, whose sprained wrist had been taped up by the doctor, managed to get on Twilight and have a trot.

"I can't believe I never even knew this trail was here," Mel said as Lauren took them down the narrow overgrown path.

"It's a little spooky," Jessica said, looking at the tall trees with their bare snow-covered branches pressing in at them.

"Yeah," Anna agreed. She shivered. "It feels like there might be ghosts or . . . oh, wow!" She gasped as the trail led into the clearing.

The moonflowers had pushed their star-shaped heads through the snow so that the grass looked like a white carpet dotted with purple stars. A pair of robin redbreasts

was flying across the clearing. They landed
on a nearby bush and, with their heads
tilted to one side, chirped at the girls. A
red squirrel crouched on the snow-covered
grass mound in the center of the clearing.
With a flick of its russet tail, it scampered

across the snow and up a tree trunk. The snow was heavy on the branches and the air had a strange, mysterious feel.

Lauren looked at her friends. Their eyes were huge in wonder.

"What an amazing place," Carla whispered.

"It feels like . . . like it's magic or something," Mel exclaimed.

Anna nodded. "Like something weird could happen."

"I love it," Jessica said softly.

Lauren stroked Twilight's neck. She'd been wondering if she was doing the right thing by bringing her friends to the clearing, but now she was very glad she had. The clearing seemed even more wonderful with all her friends there to share it.

They stayed for a while and then, leaving the clearing to the squirrel and the robins, they headed back to the farmhouse. Mrs. Foster was waiting with a delicious brunch of pancakes, hot chocolate, and Christmas muffins.

After brunch, they got the ponies ready for the show.

"I'm going to miss being here," Carla said as she helped Mel wash Shadow's tail.

"You'll have to come back," Mel told her.

"Yeah, when it's warmer," Jessica put in. "Then we can go for a picnic together."

"Or if you came at Easter, we could go for an Easter egg hunt," Mel said.

"Cool!" Anna said. "Can we do that, Lauren?"

"Of course," Lauren said happily. "That would be great!"

The next day, Carla and Anna were up early with Lauren. They helped her muck out and give Twilight a final brush over before the show. They had just finished decorating his bridle with tinsel when Anna's dad arrived.

There was a flurry of activity as they loaded up their bags and thanked Lauren's parents. Then Carla and Anna got into the car.

"Good luck at the show!" Carla called.

"Call us and tell us how it went," Anna said.

"I will," Lauren promised. "See you at Easter!"

She waved them off and five minutes later, Mel's mom arrived with the horse trailer and Mel and Jessica.

"Hi, Lauren!" Mel shouted, rolling down the window.

"Are you ready for the show?" Jessica cried.

Lauren grinned. "You bet!"

Despite their disastrous practice on Monday, Mel, Lauren, and Jessica won five team ribbons in the show — a fourth in the bending, a third in the potato race, a second in the walk, trot, and gallop, and two firsts in the sack race and the relay. In fact, they won so many ribbons that they were awarded the prize for best team age ten years and under.

After they had each been presented with a small silver badge, they galloped around the indoor arena with the tune of "We Wish You a Merry Christmas" booming out through the loudspeakers. Lauren didn't think she'd ever felt happier. She could see it was starting to snow again outside, it was Christmas Day tomorrow, and she had the best friends in the world — old ones, new ones, and, of course, one very special one.

When they rode out of the ring, Mel and Jessica went over to Mel's mom but Lauren reined Twilight in. Listening to the Christmas music playing in the background, she dismounted and hugged him.

Twilight snorted softly.

Lauren kissed his neck. Even though he wasn't a unicorn right then, she knew just what he was saying.

"Merry Christmas to you, too, Twilight," she whispered.

For a moment they stood there with snowflakes falling all around them and then, smiling happily, Lauren led him over to join the others.